Algernon Charles Swinburne

Rosamund, Queen of the Lombards

A tradegy

Algernon Charles Swinburne

Rosamund, Queen of the Lombards
A tradegy

ISBN/EAN: 9783337329204

Printed in Europe, USA, Canada, Australia, Japan

Cover: Foto ©Andreas Hilbeck / pixelio.de

More available books at **www.hansebooks.com**

ROSAMUND,

Queen of the Lombards

A TRAGEDY

By Algernon Charles Swinburne

NEW YORK

Dodd, Mead & Company, 1899

D. B. Updike, The Merrymount Press, Boston

.

PERSONS REPRESENTED

ALBOVINE, *King of the Lombards.*

ALMACHILDES, *a young Lombard warrior.*

NARSETES, *an old leader and counsellor.*

ROSAMUND, *Queen of the Lombards.*

HILDEGARD, *a noble Lombard maiden.*

SCENE, *Verona.*

TIME, *June 573.*

ROSAMUND,

QUEEN OF THE LOMBARDS

ACT I

A Hall in the Palace: a curtain drawn midway across it.

Enter ALBOVINE *and* NARSETES.

ALBOVINE.

THIS is no matter of the wars: in war
Thy king, old friend, is less than king of thine,
And comrade less than follower. Hast thou loved
Ever—loved woman, not as chance may love,
But as thou hast loved thy sword or friend—or me?
Thou hast shewn me love more stout of heart than death
Death quailed before thee when thou gav'st me life,
Borne down in battle.

NARSETES.

Woman? As I love
Flowers in their season. A rose is but a rose.

ALBOVINE.

Dost thou know rose from thistle or bindweed? Man,

Speak as our north wind speaks, if harsh and hard —

Truth.

NARSETES.

White I know from red, and dark from bright,

And milk from blood in hawthorn-flowers: but not

Woman from woman.

ALBOVINE.

How should God our Lord,

Except his eye see further than his world?

For women ever make themselves anew,

Meseems, to match and mock the maker. Friend,

If ever I were friend of thine in fight,

Speak, and I bid thee not speak truth: I know

Thy tongue knows nought but truth or silence.

NARSETES.

Is it

A king's or friend's part, king, to bid his friend

Speak what he knows not? Speak then thou, that I

May find thy will and answer it.

ALBOVINE.

I am fain

And loth to tell thee how it wrings my heart

That now this hard-eyed heavy southern sun

Hath wrought its will upon us all a year

And yet I know not if my wife be mine.

NARSETES.

Thy meanest man at arms had known ere dawn

Blinked on his bridal birthday.

ALBOVINE.

Did I bid thee

Mock, and forget me for thy friend — I say not,

King? Is thy heart so light and lean a thing,

So loose in faith and faint in love? I bade thee

Stand to me, help me, hold my hand in thine

And give my heart back answer. This it is,

Old friend and fool, that gnaws my life in twain —

The worm that writhes and feeds about my heart —

The devil and God are crying in either ear

One murderous word for ever, night and day,

Dark day and deadly night and deadly day,

Can she love thee who slewest her father? I

Love her.

NARSETES.

Thy wife should love thee as thy sire's

Loved him. Thou art worth a woman — heart for heart.

ALBOVINE.

My sire's wife loved him? Hers he had not slain.

Would God I might but die and burn in hell

And know my love had loved me!

NARSETES.

Is thy name

Babe? Sweet are babes as flowers that wed the sun,

But man may be not born a babe again,

And less than man may woman. Rosamund

Stands radiant now in royal pride of place

As wife of thine and queen of Lombards — not

Cunimund's daughter. Hadst thou slain her sire

Shamefully, shame were thine to have sought her hand

And shame were hers to love thee: but he died

Manfully, by thy mightier hand than his
Manfully mastered. War, born blind as fire,
Fed not as fire upon her: many a maid
As royal dies disrobed of all but shame
And even to death burnt up for shame's sake: she
Lives, by thy grace, imperial.

ALBOVINE.
                              He or I,
Her lord or sire, which hath most part in her,
This hour shall try between us.

Enter ROSAMUND.

ROSAMUND.
                              Royal lord,
Thy wedded handmaid craves of thee a grace.

ALBOVINE.
My sovereign bids her bondman what she will.

ROSAMUND.
I bid thee mock me not: I may ask thee
Aught, and be heard of any save my lord.

ALBOVINE.

Go. friend.

[*Exit* NARSETES.

Speak now. Say first what ails thee?

ROSAMUND.

Me?

ALBOVINE.

Thy voice was honey-hearted music, sweet
As wine and glad as clarions: not in battle
Might man have more of joy than I to hear it
And feel delight dance in my heart and laugh
Too loud for hearing save its own. Thou rose,
Why did God give thee more than all thy kin
Whose pride is perfume only and colour, this?
Music? No rose but mine sings, and the birds
Hush all their hearts to hearken. Dost thou hear not
How heavy sounds her note now?

ROSAMUND.

Sire, not I.

But sire I should not call thee.

ALBOVINE.

Surely, no.

I bade thee speak: I did not bid thee sing:

Thou canst not speak and sing not.

ROSAMUND.

Albovine,

I had at heart a simple thing to crave

And thought not on thy flatteries—as I think not

Now. Knowest thou not my handmaid Hildegard

Free-born, a noble maiden?

ALBOVINE.

And a fair

As ever shone like sundawn on the snows.

ROSAMUND.

I had at heart to plead for her with thee.

ALBOVINE.

Plead? hast thou found her noble maidenhood

Ignobly turned unmaidenlike? I may not

Lightly believe it.

ROSAMUND.

Believe it not at all.

Wouldst thou think shame of me — lightly? She loves

As might a maid whose kin were northern gods

The fairest-faced of warriors Lombard born,

Thine Almachildes.

ALBOVINE.

If he loves not her,

More fool is he than warrior even, though war

Have wakened laughter in his eyes, and left

His golden hair fresh gilded, when his hand

Had won the crown that clasps a boy's brows close

With first-born sign of battle.

ROSAMUND.

No such fool

May live in such a warrior; if he love not

Some loveliness not hers. No face as bright

Crowned with so fair a Mayflower crown of praise

Lacked ever yet love, if its eyes were set

With all their soul to loveward.

ALBOVINE.

Ay?

ROSAMUND.

I know not

A man so fair of face. I like him well.

And well he hath served and loves thee.

ALBOVINE.

Ay? The boy

Seems winsome then with women.

ROSAMUND.

Hildegard

Hath hearkened when he spake of love — it may be,

Lightly.

ALBOVINE.

To her shall no man lightly speak.

Thy maiden and our natural kin is she.

Wilt thou speak with him — lightly?

ROSAMUND.

If thou wilt,

Gladly.

ALBOVINE.

The boy shall wait upon thy will.   [*Exit.*

ROSAMUND.

My heart is heavier than this heat that weighs

With all the weight of June on us. I know not

Why. And the feast is close on us. I would

This night were now to-morrow morn. I know not

Why.

Enter ALMACHILDES.

Ah! What would you?

ALMACHILDES.

Queen, our lord the king

Bade me before thee hither.

ROSAMUND.

Truth : I know it.

Thou art loved and honoured of our lord the king.

Dost thou, whom honour loves before thy time,

Love?

ALMACHILDES.

Ay: thy noble handmaid, Hildegard.

I know not if she love me.

ROSAMUND.

Thou shalt know.

But this thou knowest : I may not give thee her.

ALMACHILDES.

I would not take her from the Lord God's hand

If hers were given against her will to mine.

ROSAMUND.

A man said that : a manfuller than men

Who grip the loveless hands of prisoners. Well

It must be with the bride whose happier hand

Lies fond and fast in thine. Our Hildegard,

Being free and noble as Albovine and we,

Born one with us in race and blood, and thence

Our equal in our sole nobility,

Must well be won by noble works, and love

Whose light is one with honour's.

ALMACHILDES.

Queen, may I

Perchance not win it? I know not.

ROSAMUND.

Nay, nor I.

Soon may we know; they are entering toward the feast.

[The curtain drawn discovers a banquet, with

guests assembled: among them NARSETES

and HILDEGARD.

Re-enter ALBOVINE.

ALBOVINE.

Thine hand: I hold the whitest in the world.

Sit thou, boy, there, beside sweet Hildegard.

[They sit.

Bring me the cup. Queen, thou shalt pledge with me

A health to all this kingdom and its weal

Even from the bowl that here to hold in hand

Assures me lord of Lombardy and thine

By right and might of battle and of God— .

The skull that was thy father's: so shalt thou

Drink to me with thy father.

ROSAMUND.

Sire, my lord,

The life my sire, who gave thee up his life,

Gave me, and fostered till thou hadst given him death,

Is all now thine. Thy will be done. I drink

To thee, who art all this kingdom and its weal,

All health and honour that of right should be,

With all good things I wish thee.   [*Drinks.*

ALBOVINE.

Wish me well,

And God must give me what thou wilt. Good friends,

My warriors and my brethren, hath not he

Given me to wife the best one born of man

And loveliest, and most loving? Silent, sirs?

Wherefore?

ROSAMUND.

Thou shouldst not ask it. Bid the cup

Go blithely round.

ALBOVINE.

By Christ and Thor, it shall.

What ails the boy there? Almachildes!

ALMACHILDES.

                              King,

Nought ails me.

ALBOVINE.

Nor thy maiden?

ALMACHILDES.

                         King, nor her.

ALBOVINE.

Fall then to feasting. Bear the cup away.

Some savour of the dust of death comes from it.

Sweet, be not wroth nor sad.

ROSAMUND.

                         I am blithe and fain,

Sire ; and I loved thee never more than now.

ALBOVINE.

Nor ever I thee. Now I find thee mine,

And now no daughter of mine enemy's.

ROSAMUND.

                              No.

Thou hast no enemy left on earth alive —

No soul unslain that hates thee.

ALBOVINE.

That were much.

What man may say it? and least of all may kings.

ROSAMUND.

What hast thou done that man should hate thee — man

Or woman?

ALBOVINE.

Which of us may answer, Nought?

ROSAMUND.

Thou might'st have made me — me, my father's child

Harlot and slave : thou hast made me wife and queen.

ALBOVINE.

Thee have I loved ; ay, and myself in thee,

Who hast made me more than king and lord, being thine.

ROSAMUND.

Courtesy sets on kings a goldener crown

That sits upon them seemlier.

ALBOVINE.

Courtesy!

Truth. Hark thee, boy, and let thy Hildegard

Hearken. Is she, thy queen, a peer of mine?

ALMACHILDES.

She wears no crown but heaven's about her head —

No gold that was not born upon her brows

Transfigures or disfigures them. She is not

A peer of thine.

ROSAMUND.

He answers well.

ALBOVINE.

He answers

Ill — as the spirit of shamelessness might speak.

ALMACHILDES.

Shameless are they that lie. I lie not.

ALBOVINE.

Boy,

Tempt not the rod.

ALMACHILDES.

The rod that man may wield

No man may fear: the slave who fears it is not

Man.

ALBOVINE.

Art thou crazed with wine?

ALMACHILDES.

Am I thy king?

ALBOVINE.

My thrall thou knowest thou art not, or thy tongue

Durst challenge not mine anger.

ROSAMUND.

Thrall and free,

Woman and man, yea, queen and king, are born

More wide apart than earth or hell and heaven.

Sirs, let no wrangling breath distune the peace

That shines and glows about us, and discerns

A banquet from a battle. Thou, my lord,

Hast bidden away the dust of death which fell

Between us at thy bidding, and is now

Nothing—a dream blown out at waking. Thou,

My lord's young chosen of warriors, be not wroth,

Albeit thy wrath be noble, though my lord

See fit to try my love as gold is tried

By fire : it burns not thee. Strike hand in hand :

Ye have done so after battle.

ALBOVINE.

               Drink again

I pledge thee, boy.

ALMACHILDES.

               I pledge thee, king.

ROSAMUND.

                      My lord,

I am weary at heart, and fain would sleep. Forgive me

That I can sit no more.

ALBOVINE.

               What ails thee ?

ROSAMUND.

                     Nought.

The hot and heavy time of year has bound

About my brows a band of iron. Sire,

Thou wouldst not see me sink aswoon, and mar

The raptures of thy revel.

ALBOVINE.

Get thee hence.

Go. God be with thee.

ROSAMUND.

God abide with thee.

[*Exit with attendants*

ALBOVINE.

This is no feast : I will no more of it. Boy,

Take note, and tempt not so thy bride, albeit

She tempt thee to the trial.

ALMACHILDES.

I shall not, king.

ALBOVINE.

She will not. Sirs, good night—if night may be

Good. Hardly may the day be, here. And yet

For you it may be — Hildegard and thee.

God give you joy.

ALMACHILDES.

God give thee comfort, king.

[Exeunt.

ACT II

Enter ROSAMUND.

ROSAMUND.

I AM yet alive to question if I live
And wonder what may ever bid me die.
But live I will, being yet not dead with thee,
Father. Thou knowest in Paradise my heart.
I feel thy kisses breathing on my lips,
Whereto the dead cold relic of thy face
Was pressed at bidding of thy slayer last night,
And yet they were not withered: nay, they are red
As blood is—blood but newly spilt—not thine.
How good thou wast and sweet of spirit—how dear,
Father! None lives that knew thee now save one,
And none loves me but thou nor thee but I,
That was till yesternight thy daughter: now
That very name is tainted, and my tongue
Tastes poison as I speak it. There is nought

Left in the range and record of the world

For me that is not poisoned: even my heart

Is all envenomed in me. Death is life,

Or priesthood lies that swears it: then I give

The man my husband and thy homicide

Life, if I slay him — the life he gave thee.

Enter HILDEGARD.

Girl,

I sent for thee, I think: stand near me. Child,

Thou art fairer than thou knowest, I doubt: thou art

    fair

As the awless maidenhood of morning: truth

Should live upon thy lips, though truth were dead

On all men's tongues and women's born save thine.

Dawn lies not when it laughs on us. Thy queen

I am not now: thy friend I would be. Tell

Thy friend if love sleep or awake in thee

Toward any man. Thou art silent. Tell me this,

Dost thou not think, where thought scarce knows it-

    self —

Think in the subtle sense too deep for thought —

That Almachildes loves thee?

HILDEGARD.

More than I

Love Almachildes.

ROSAMUND.

Thus a maid should speak.

Dost thou love me?

HILDEGARD.

Thou knowest it, queen.

ROSAMUND.

It lies

Now in thy power to show me more of love

Than ever yet hath man or woman. Swear,

If thou dost love me, thou wilt show it.

HILDEGARD.

I swear.

ROSAMUND.

By all our fathers' great forsaken gods

Who smiled on all their battles, and by him

Who clomb or crept or leapt upon their throne

And signed us Christian, swear it, then.

HILDEGARD.

I swear

ROSAMUND.

What if I bid thee give thyself to shame —

Yield up thy soul and body — play such parts

As shameless fame records of women crowned

Imperial in the tale of lust and Rome?

HILDEGARD.

Thou couldst not bid me do it.

ROSAMUND.

Thou hast sworn.

HILDEGARD.

I have sworn.

Queen, I would do it, and die.

ROSAMUND.

Thou shalt not. Yet

This must thou do, and live. Thou shalt not be

Shamed. Thou shalt bid thine Almachildes come

And speak with thee by nightfall. Say, the queen

Will give not up the maiden so beloved

—And truth it is, I love thee— willingly

To the arms of one her husband loves: but were it .

Shame, utter shame, that he should wed not her,

The shamefast·queen could choose not. Then shall he

Plead. Then shalt thou turn gentler than the snow

That softens at the strong sun's kiss, and yield.

But needs must night be close about your love

And darkness whet your kisses. Light were death.

Hast thou no heart to guess now? Fear not then.

Not thou but I must put on shame. I lack

A hand for mine to grasp and strike with. His

I have chosen.

HILDEGARD.

I see but as by lightning. Queen,

What should I do but warn the king—or him?

ROSAMUND.

Thou hast sworn. I hold thee by thy word.

HILDEGARD.

                          My Christ,

Help me!

ROSAMUND.

    No God can break thine oath in twain

And leave thee less than perjured. Thou must bid him

Make thee to-night his bride.

HILDEGARD.

                  I could not say it.

ROSAMUND.

Thou shalt, or God shall smite thee down to hell.

What, art thou godless?

HILDEGARD.

              Art not thou?

ROSAMUND.

                            Not I.

I find him just and gracious, girl: he gives me

My right by might set fast on thine and thee.

HILDEGARD.

For love of mercy, queen — for honour's sake,

Bid me not shame myself before a man —

The man I love — who gives me back at least

Honour, if love he gives not.

ROSAMUND.

Ay, my maid?

And yet he loves thee, or thy maiden thought

Errs with no gracious error, more than thou

Him?

HILDEGARD.

Art thou woman born, to cast me back

My maiden shame for shame upon my face?

I would not say I loved him more than man

Loved ever woman since the light of love

Lit them alive together. Let us be.

ROSAMUND.

I will not. Mine are both by God's own gift.

I will not cast it from me. Ye may live

Hereafter happy: never now shall I.

HILDEGARD.

Have mercy. Nay, I cannot do it. And thou,

Albeit thine heart be hot with hate as hell,

Couldst say not, nor fold round with fairer speech,

Those foul three words the Egyptian woman said

Who tempted and could tempt not Joseph.

ROSAMUND.
                                        No.

He would not hearken. Joseph loved not her

More than thine Almachildes me. But thou

Shalt. Now no more may I debate with thee.

Go.

HILDEGARD.

God requite thee!

ROSAMUND.

                    That shall he and I,

Not thou, make proof of. If I plead with him,

I crave of God but wrong's requital. Go.

                         [*Exit* HILDEGARD.

And yet, God help me! Can I do it? God's will

May no man thwart, or leave his righteousness

Baffled. I would not say, 'My will be done,'

Were God's will not for righteousness as mine,

If right be righteous, wrong be wrong, must be.

How else may God work wrong's requital? I

Must be or none may be his minister.

And yet what righteousness is his to cast

Athwart my way toward right this wrong to me,

A sin against the soul and honour? Why

Must this vile word of *yet* cross all my thought

Always, a drifting doom or doubt that still

Strikes up and floats against my purpose? God,

Help me to know it! This weapon chosen of me,

This Almachildes, were his face not fair,

Were not his fame bright — were his aspect foul,

His name dishonourable, his line through life

A loathing and a spitting-stock for scorn,

Could I do this? Am I then even as they

Who queened it once in Rome's abhorrent face

An empress each, and each by right of sin

Prostitute? All the life I have lived or loved

Hath been, if snows or seas or wellsprings be,

Pure as the spirit of love toward heaven is — chaste

As children's eyes or mothers'. Though I sinned

As yet my soul hath sinned not, Albovine

Must bear, if God abhor unrighteousness,

The weight of penance heaviest laid on sin,

Shame. Not on me may shame be set, though hell

Take hold upon me dying. I would the deed

Were done, the wreak of wrath were wroken, and I

Dead.

Enter ALBOVINE.

ALBOVINE.

Art thou sick at heart to see me ?

ROSAMUND.

No.

ALBOVINE.

Thou art sweet and wise as ever God hath made

Woman. I would not turn thine heart from me

Or set thy spirit against the sense of mine

For more than Rome's old empire.

ROSAMUND.

That, albeit

Thou wouldst, be sure thou canst not. God nor man

Could wake within me toward my lord the king

A new strange love or loathing. Fear not this.

ALBOVINE.

From thee can I fear nothing. Now I know

How high thy heart is, and how true to me.

ROSAMUND.

Thou knowest it now.

ALBOVINE.

                     I know not if I should

Repent me, or repent not, that I tried

A heart so high so sorely—proved so true.

ROSAMUND.

Do not repent. I would not have thee now

Repent.

ALBOVINE.

          By Christ, if God forbade it not,

I would have said within mine own fool's heart,

Of all vile things that fool the soul of man

The vilest and the priestliest hath to name

Repentance. Could it blot one hour's work out,

A wise thing and a manful thing it were,

And profit were it none for priests to preach.

This will I tell thee : what last night befell

Rejoices not but irks me.

ROSAMUND.

Let it not

Rejoice nor irk thee. Vex thou not thy soul

With any thought thereon, if none may bid thee

Rejoice : and that were harsh and hard of heart.

ALBOVINE.

I will not. Queen and wife, hell durst not say

I do not love thee.

ROSAMUND.

Heaven has heard — and I.

ALBOVINE.

Forget then all this foolishness, and pray

God may forget it.

ROSAMUND.

God forgets as I.   [*Exit* ALBOVINE.

And had repentance helped him? Shall I think

It might have molten in my burning heart

The thrice-retempered iron of resolve?

Yet well it is to know that penitence

Lies further from that frozen heart of his

Than mercy from the tiger's. Ay, God knows,

I had scorned him too had penitence bowed him down

Before me : now I do but hate. I am not

Abased as wholly, so supremely shamed,

As though I had wedded one as hard as he

Who yet might think to soften down with words

What hardly might be cleansed with tears of blood,

The monumental memory graven on steel

That burns the naked spirit of sense within me

Like the ardent sting of keen-edged ice, which makes

The naked flesh feel fire upon it.

Enter ALMACHILDES.

ALMACHILDES.

.   Queen,

I come to crave a word of thee.

ROSAMUND.

I hear.

ALMACHILDES.

Thou knowest I love thy noble Hildegard :

And rather would I give my soul to burn

Than wrong in thought her flawless maidenhood.

And now she hath told me what I dare not think

Truth. And I dare not think her lips may lie.

ROSAMUND.

I have heard. And what is this to me? She hath not

Said—hath not told thee, nor wouldst thou believe—

That I have breathed a lie upon her lips

Or taught them shamelessness by lesson?

ALMACHILDES.

No.

But she came forth from thee to me—from thee—

And spake with quivering mouth and quailing eyes

And face whose fire turned ashen, and again

Rekindling from that ashen agony

Flamed, what no heart could think to hear her speak,

Mine least of all, who love her.

ROSAMUND.

Ay?

ALMACHILDES.

Not she,

I know it as sure as night is known from day

And surelier than I know mine own soul's truth,

Spake what she spake in broken bursts of breath

Out of her own heart and its love for me.

ROSAMUND.

Didst thou so answer her?

ALMACHILDES.

I might not well

Answer at all.

ROSAMUND.

Poor maid, she hath loved amiss.

Belike she thought to find in thee a man's

Love.

ALMACHILDES.

That she hath found; nought meaner than a man's;

No wolfish lust of ravenous insolence

To soil and spoil her of her noblest name.

ROSAMUND.

I do not ask thee what she said. I know.

ALMACHILDES.

I knew thou didst.

ROSAMUND.

To make your bridal sure
She bade thee make thy bride of her to-night.

ALMACHILDES.

She bade me as a slave might bid the scourge
Fall.

ROSAMUND.

Such a scourge no slave might shrink from ; nay,
No free-born woman, Almachildes.

ALMACHILDES.

Queen,
I crave thy queenly mercy though I say
My maid, my bride that will be, shrank, and showed
In all the rosebright anguish of her face
A shuddering shame that wrung my heart. And thou
Hast surely set thereon that seal of shame.
I know it as thou dost.

ROSAMUND.

Ay, and more she said,

Surely : she said I would not yield her up

To the arms of one my husband loves and holds

Honoured at heart — I hate my husband so,

She told thee — were the need avoidable

Save by her sacrifice to shame.

ALMACHILDES.

Thou knowest

All, as I knew, and lacked not from thy lips

Confession.

ROSAMUND.

Warrior though thou be, and boy

Though my lord call thee, brainless art thou not

No sword with man's face carven on the heft

For mockery more than truth or help in fight.

I do not and I durst not play with thee.

Thy bride spake truth: I knew not she might need

So much of truth to tempt thee toward her. Now

Thou knowest, and I know. If this imminent night

Make not thy darkling bride of her, by day

Thy bride she may be never. She hath sworn.

ALMACHILDES.

Why wouldst thou shame her?

ROSAMUND.

           Shamed she cannot be

If thou be found not shameless. Plead no more

Against thine own love's surety. Doubt thou not

I wish thee well, and love her. Make not thou

Out of her shamefast maidenhood and fear

A sword to cleave your happiness in twain.

What if some oath constrain me, sworn in haste,

Infrangible for shame's sake, sealed in heaven

Inevitable? Ask now no more of me.

Nightfall is here upon us. Nought on earth

May set the season of your bridal back

If thou be true as she must. Wait awhile

Here till a sign be sent thee — till a bell

Strike softly from this chamber here at hand.

I have sworn to her she shall not see thy face.

So sore she prayed she might not : and for thee

I swore that ere the darkling air grew grey

Thou shouldst arise and leave her, and behold

Thy midnight bride but when thou art bidden again

To meet her here to-morrow. Strange it were,

More strange than aught of all, that thou shouldst prove

Dishonourable : and except thou be, these things

Must all be wrought in this wise, lest her oath

And mine, at peril of her soul and life,

By passionate forgetfulness of thine

Disloyally be broken. Swear to us now

Thou wilt not break our oath and thine, or think

. To look to-night upon thy bride.

ALMACHILDES.

                          I swear.

ROSAMUND.

I take thine oath. I bid not thee take heed

That I or thou or each of us at once,

Couldst thou play false, may die : I bid thee think

Thy bride will die, shamed. Swear me not again

She shall not : all our trust is set on thee.

What eyes and ears are keen about us here

Thou knowest not. Love, my love and thine for her,

Shall deafen and shall blind them. Be but thou

A bridegroom blind and dumb—speak soft as love,

And ask not answer louder than a sigh —

And when to-morrow sets thy bride and thee

Here face to face again, thy soul shall stand

Amazed : thy joy shall turn to wonder. This

Thy queen, whose power may seal her promise fast,

Swears for thine oath again to thee. Good night.

[*Exit.*

ALMACHILDES.

I cannot think I live. Our Sigurd loved not

Brynhild as I love her, and even this hour

Shall make us great as they. No spell to break,

No fire to pass, divides us. Blind and dumb,

Love knows, would I be ever while I live

For love's sake rather than forego the joy

That makes one godlike power of spirit and sense,

One godhead born of manhood. God requite

The queen who loves my love and cares for me

Thus! How may man or God requite her? Ah!

      [*Bell rings softly from within.*

There sounds the note that opens heaven on me,

And how should man dare heaven? But love may dare.

         [*Exit.*

ACT III

An eastward room in the Palace.

Enter ALBOVINE.

ALBOVINE.

THIS sun — no sun like ours — burns out my soul.
    I would, when June takes hold on us like fire,
The wind could waft and whirl us northward : here
The splendour and the sweetness of the world
Eat out all joy of life or manhood. Earth
Is here too hard on heaven — the Italian air
Too bright to breathe, as fire, its next of kin,
Too keen to handle. God, whoe'er God be,
Keep us from withering as the lords of Rome —
Slackening and sickening toward the imperious end
That wiped them out of empire! Yea, he shall.

Enter HILDEGARD.

HILDEGARD.

The queen would wait upon your majesty.

ALBOVINE.

Bid her come in. And tell her ere she come

I wait upon her will.

[*Exit* HILDEGARD.

What would she now?

Enter ROSAMUND.

By Christ, how fair thou art! I never saw thee

So like the sun in heaven : no rose on earth

Might think to match thee.

ROSAMUND.

All I am is thine.

ALBOVINE.

Mine? God might come from heaven to worship thee.

Thine eyes outlighten all the stars : thy face

Leaves earth no flower to worship.

ROSAMUND.

How should earth

Worship her children? Nought it is in me,

My lord's dear love it is, that makes me seem

Fair.

ALBOVINE.

How thou liest thou knowest not. Rosamund,

What hast thou done to be so beautiful ?

ROSAMUND.

The sun has left thine eyes half blind.

ALBOVINE.

                        I dare not

Kiss thee, or stare straight-eyed against the sun.

ROSAMUND.

Kiss me. Who knows how long the lord of life

May spare us time for kissing ? Life and love

Are less than change and death.

ALBOVINE.

                   What ghosts are they ?

So sweet thou never wast to me before.

The woman that is God — the God that is

Woman — the sovereign of the soul of man,

Our fathers' Freia, Venus crowned in Rome,

Has lent my love her girdle ; but her lips

Have robbed the red rose of its heart, and left

No glory for the flower beyond all flowers

To bid the spring be glad of.

ROSAMUND.

Summer and spring

May cleanse and heal the heart of man no more

Than winter may, or withering autumn. Sire,

Husband and lord, I have a woful word

To speak against a man beloved of thee,

A man well worth all glory man may give —

Against thine Almachildes.

ALBOVINE.

Has the boy

Transgressed again in lawless heat of speech

And kindled wrath in thee against him — thee,

Who stood'st between my wrath and him?

ROSAMUND.

I would

His were no more transgression than of speech.

He hath wronged — I bid thee ask of me no more —

A noble maiden. Till her shame be healed,

Her name is dead upon my lips and his,

Who is yet not all ignoble.

ALBOVINE.

He shall die

Except he wed her, and she will to wed.

ROSAMUND.

That surely will she.

ALBOVINE.

Bid him hither.

ROSAMUND.

See,

There strides he through the sunshine toward the shade.

How light and high he steps! He sees thee. Bid him—

Beckon him in.

ALBOVINE.

He knows mine eye. He comes.

ROSAMUND.

Obedient as a hound is.

ALBOVINE.

As a man

That knows the law of loyal manhood.

ROSAMUND.

Ay?

God send it be so.

Enter ALMACHILDES.

ALMACHILDES.

Queen and king, I am here.

What would you?

ALBOVINE.

Truth. Hast thou not borne thyself

Toward any soul on earth disloyally

Ever?

ALMACHILDES.

Never.

ALBOVINE.

I would not say thou liest.

ALMACHILDES.

Do not: the lie should burn thy lips up, king.

ALBOVINE.

Thou hast wrought no wrong toward man or woman?

ALMACHILDES.

None.

ALBOVINE.

Speak thou: thou hast heard him answer me.

ROSAMUND.

I have heard.

No wrong it may be with the serfs of hell

To cast upon a woman for a curse

Shame: to defile the spirit and shrine of love,

Put out the sunlike eyes of maidenhood

And leave the soul dismantled. Has not he

So sinned ?— Hast thou wrought no such work as this?

The king has heard thy silence.

ALMACHILDES.

Queen and king.

I have done no wrong, but right. I have chosen my bride,

And made her mine by gentle grace of hers

Lest wrong should come between us. Now no man

May think to unwed us: king nor queen may cross

This wedded love of ours: no thwart or stay

May sunder us till heaven and earth turn hell.

ALBOVINE.

I deemed not thee dishonourable: and thy queen

Now knows thee true as I did. Rosamund,

Forgive and give him back his bride.

ROSAMUND.

I will,

King.

ALBOVINE.

Boy, thy queen hath shown thee grace; be thou

Thankful. I leave thee here to yield her thanks.

[*Exit.*

ALMACHILDES.

Queen, I would die to serve and thank thee.

ROSAMUND.

Die?

So young and glad and glorious? Thou shalt not

Die. Was thy bride's face bright to look upon

When last night's moon and stars illumined it?

ALMACHILDES.

Thou knowest I might not look upon it.

ROSAMUND.

No.

Thou hast never loved before?

ALMACHILDES.

     I have loathed, not loved,

The loveless harlots clasped of all the camp:

I have followed wars and visions all my days

Even till my love's eyes lit and stung to life

The soul within my body. Till I loved,

I knew not woman.

ROSAMUND.

    Now thou knowest. This love

Is no good lord — no gentle god — no soft

Saviour. Thou knowest perchance thy bride's name —

   hers

Whose body and soul were one but now with thine?

ALMACHILDES.

How should not I? What darkling light is this

That burns and broods and lightens in thine eyes,

Queen?

ROSAMUND.

Hildegard it was not.

ALMACHILDES.

     Art not thou —

Or am not I—sun-smitten through the brain

By this mad might of midsummer? Who was it

That slept or slept not with me while the night

Was more than noon and more than heaven? What name

Was hers who made me godlike?

ROSAMUND.

Rosamund.

ALMACHILDES.

Thine? Was it thou? It was not.

ROSAMUND.

It was I.

ALMACHILDES.

Does the sun stand in heaven? Or stands it fast

As when God bade it halt on high? My life

Is broken in me.

ROSAMUND.

Nay, fair sir, not yet.

Thy life is now mine—as the ring I wear

That seals my hand a wife's. Die thou shalt not,

But slay, and live.

ALMACHILDES.

Slay whom?

ROSAMUND.

               Thy lord and mine.

ALMACHILDES.

I had rather go down quick to hell.

ROSAMUND.

                  I know it.

I leave thee not the choice. Keep thou thy hand

Bloodless, and Hildegard, whom yet I love,

Dies, and in fire, the harlot's death of shame.

Last night she lured thee hither. Hate of me,

Because of late I smote her, being in wrath

Forgetful of her noble maidenhood,

Stung her for shame's sake to take hands with shame.

This if I swear, may she unswear it? Thou

Canst not but say she bade thee seek her. She

Lives while I will, as Albovine and thou

Live by my grace and mercy. Live, or die.

But live thou shalt not longer than her death,

Her death by burning, if thou slay not him.

I see my death shine in thine eyes: I see

My present death inflame them. That were not

Her surety, Almachildes. Thou shouldst know me

Now. Though thou slay me, this may save not her.

My lines are laid about her life, and may not

By breach of mine be broken.

ALMACHILDES.

God must be

Dead. Such a thing as thou could never else

Live.

ROSAMUND.

That concerns not thee nor me. Be thou

Sure that my will and power to serve it live.

Lift now thine eyes to look upon thy lord.

Re-enter ALBOVINE.

ALBOVINE.

By this time hath he thanked thee not enough?

ROSAMUND.

More hath he given than thanks.

ALBOVINE.

What more may be ?

ROSAMUND.

His plighted faith to heal the wrong he wrought

Faithfully.

ALBOVINE.

Boy, strike then thy hand in mine.

Thou art loyal as I knew thee.

ALMACHILDES.

King, I may not

Touch hands with thee.

ALBOVINE.

Thou art false, then, ha ? Thou hast lied ?

ALMACHILDES.

King, till the wrong I have wrought be wreaked or

healed

I clasp not hands with honour. Nay, and then   .

Perchance I may not.

ALBOVINE.

Boy I called thee: child

I call thee now. But, boy, the child thou art

Is noble as our sires.

ALMACHILDES.

Would God it were!

[*Exit.*

ALBOVINE.

What ails him?

ROSAMUND.

Love and shame.

ALBOVINE.

No more than these?

ROSAMUND.

Enough are they to darken death and life.

ALBOVINE.

Thou art less than gentle towards his love and him.

ROSAMUND.

I would not speak ungently. Her I love,

Poor child, and him I hate not.

ALBOVINE.

Thou shalt live

To love him too.

ROSAMUND.

This heaviness of heat

Kills love and hate and life in me. I know not

Ought lovesome save the sweet brief death of sleep.

ALBOVINE.

I am weary as thou. Good night we may not say—

Good noon I bid thee. Sleep shall heal us.

ROSAMUND.

                            Ay;

No healing and no help for life on earth

Hath God or man found out save death and sleep.

                                 [*Exeunt.*

ACT IV

The same Scene.

Enter ALMACHILDES *and* HILDEGARD.

HILDEGARD.

Hast thou forgiven me?

ALMACHILDES.

    I have not forgiven

God.

HILDEGARD.

  Wilt thou slay thy soul and mine?

ALMACHILDES.

      Wilt thou

Madden me? God hath given us up to her

Who is deadlier than the fiery fang of death —

Us, innocent and loyal.

HILDEGARD.

    Nay, if I

Forgive her love of thee — though this be hard,

Canst thou forgive not?

ALMACHILDES.

Sweet, for thee and me

Remains no rescue save by death or flight

From worse than flight or death is.

HILDEGARD.

Worse is nought

But shame: and how may shame take hold on us,

On us who have sinned not? Me she bound to play thee

False, and betray thee to her arms: I might not

Choose, though my heart should rend itself in twain

And cleave with ravenous anguish: yet I live.

Vex not thy soul too sorely: me, not her,

Thy spirit embraced, thine arms and lips made thine

Me, not my darkling wraith, my changeling foe,

My thief of love, our traitress. This I bid thee,

Forget thy fear and shame to have wronged me: night

Breeds treacherous dreams that can but poison day

If thought be found so base a fool as dares

Fear. Did I doubt thy love of me, I durst not

Live or look back upon thee.

ALMACHILDES.

Wilt thou then

Fly?

HILDEGARD.

Dost thou know what flight means—thou?

It means

Fear. And is fear a new-born friend of thine?

ALMACHILDES.

God help us! if he live, and hate not man—

If Satan be not God. We will not fly.

Enter ALBOVINE *and* ROSAMUND.

ALBOVINE.

Fly? What should love at height of happiness

Or youth at height of honour fear and fly?

Would ye take wing for heaven? take shame on earth

To wed in peace and honour?

ALMACHILDES.

No, my king.

No, surely.

ROSAMUND.

Weep not, maiden. Dost not thou,

Man, that we thought her bridegroom sealed of love,

Love her?

ALMACHILDES.

No saint loved ever God as I

Her.

ROSAMUND.

And betray her to shame thou wouldst not ? See,

My lord, the silent answer flash aloud

From cheek and eye a goodly witness. Thou,

My maiden, dost thou love not him ? Nay, speak.

HILDEGARD.

I cannot say it — I cannot strive to say.

ROSAMUND.

Thou shalt. Are all we not fast bound in love —

My lord and thine, my maiden and her queen,

A fourfold chain of faith twice linked of love ?

Speak : let not shame find place where shame is none.

HILDEGARD.

I will not. King and queen and God shall hear.

I love him as our songs of old time say

Men have been loved of women akin to gods

By blood as they by spirit, albeit in me

Nought lives that woman or man or God could say

Were worth his love, if mine by grace of love

Be found not all unworthy. Mine am I

No more : mine own in no wise now, but his

To save or slay, to cherish or cast out,

Crown and discrown, abase and comfort. Shame

Were more to me than honour if his will

It were that shame should clothe me round, and life

Were the only death left fearful if he bade me

Die. Could his love be turned from me. and set

On one less loving but more fair than I,

A thrall more base than treason or a queen

Too high for shame to brand her shameful, even

Though sin had stamped and signed her foul as fraud

And loathsome as a masked adulterous lie,

Hers would I make him if I might, and yield

To her the hatefullest of hell-born things

The man found lovelier by my love than heaven.

ROSAMUND.

Great love is this to brag of: great and strange.

HILDEGARD.

Love is no braggart : lust and fraud and hate

Vaunt their vile strength when shame unveils them :
    love

Vaunts not itself. I spake not uncompelled,

And blushed not out the avowal.

ALBOVINE.

Boy, I held

And hold thee noblest of my lords of war,

And worthier than thine elders born and tried

Ere battle found thee ripe and glad at heart

To stem and swim the tide of spears : but this

I know not if thou be or any man

Be worthy of.

ALMACHILDES.

Of all men born on earth

I am most unworthy of it. None might be

Worthy.

ROSAMUND.

He weeps : thy boy is humble.

ALMACHILDES.

Queen,

I weep not. Shamed with no ignoble shame

Thou seest me : but I weep not. Yea, God knows,

Humbled I am, and humble ; not to thee.

ALBOVINE.

Chafe not : and thou, queen though thou be, and mine,

Tempt not a true man's wrath with words that bear

Fangs keener than thou knowest of.

ROSAMUND.

King, henceforth,

Being warned, I will not. Dangerous as the sea

A true man's wrath is—and a true man's love :

A woman's hath no peril in it : her tears

Wash wrath and peril away.

ALBOVINE.

I have never seen thee

Weep.

ROSAMUND.

How should I weep--I, thy wife?

ALBOVINE.

I have heard thee

Laugh; and thy smiles were always bright as fire.

ROSAMUND.

Well were it with me—ay, and reason found

For me to live and do the living world

Some service—could my husband warm thereat

His heart as winter-stricken hands in frost

Are warmed at winter fires.

ALBOVINE.

No need, no need:

The sun thou art warms all our year with love,

And leaves no chill on winter.

ROSAMUND.

Albovine,

Love now secludes us not from sight of man

From sight of this my maiden and the man

Who shines but as the battle's boy for thee

But lives for me my maiden's lover—true

As truth is—Almachildes.

ALBOVINE.

How thy lips

Hang lingering on his name as though 't were thou

That loved him! Thou shouldst love thy maiden well.

ROSAMUND.

As she loves me I love her. Hildegard,

Leave us. Thou knowest I love thee.

HILDEGARD.

Queen, I know. [Exit.

ALBOVINE.

What ails the boy? what rapturous agony

Torments and glorifies his glance at her

As with delight in torture? Cheer thee, man :

Thou art not thus all unworthy.

ROSAMUND.

Spare him, king.

A king may guess not how a man's heart yearns

With all unkingly sense of love and shame

Not all unmanly.

ALBOVINE.

Shame is none to be

Loved, and to deem that love exceeds our due

Who may not well deserve it. Sick at heart

He seems, and should be gladder than the sea

When wind and sun strike life in it.

ALMACHILDES.

I am not

So stricken, king. I thank thy care of me.

ALBOVINE.

Heart-stricken or shame-stricken art thou?

ROSAMUND.

King,

Spare him. Thou knowest not love like his. It burns

And rends and wrings the spirit.

ALBOVINE.

No. And thou,

Dost thou then?

ROSAMUND.

Eyes and heart and sense are mine

As weak and strong as woman's can but be ;

As weak in strength and strong in weakness. Men,

Being wise, and mightier than their mates on earth,

Need no such knowledge born of inborn pain,

As quickens all the spirit of sense in us.

Worms know what eagles know not.

ALBOVINE.

Like enough.

Rede me no redes and riddles. Never yet

I have loved thee more, and yet I have loved thee well,

Than now that loving-kindness borne toward love

Makes thee so gracious, pleading for it.

ROSAMUND.

Love

Sees all things lovely : thine, if praise there be,

Not mine the praise is : thee, not me, these twain

Must love and worship as their lord of love.

ALBOVINE.

Well, God be good to them and thee and me !

I would this fierce Italian June were dead,

So hard it weighs upon me.

ROSAMUND.

Now not long

Shall we sustain or sink aswoon from it :

It has but left a day or two to die.

ALBOVINE.

And well were that, if summer died with June.

Two red months more must set on sense and soul

The branding-iron stamped of summer : nay,

The sea is here no sea to cherish man :

It brings no choral comfort back with tides

That surge and sink and swell and chime and change

And lighten life with music where the breath

Dies and revives of night and day.

ROSAMUND.

Be thou

Content : a God hath driven us hither.

ALBOVINE.

Yea :

A God of death and fire and strife, whose hand

Is heavy on my spirit. Be not ye

Troubled, if peace be with you.

ROSAMUND.

Peace to thee.

[*Exit* ALBOVINE.

Now follow: smite him now: thou art strong, but yet

Thy king is stronger—mightier thewed than thou.

Thou couldst not slay him in fight.

ALMACHILDES.

I cannot slay him

Thus.

ROSAMUND.

Canst thou slay thy bride by fire ? He dies,

Or she dies, bound against the stake. His death

Were the easier. Follow him: save her: strike but once.

ALMACHILDES.

I cannot. God requite thee this ! I will.　　　[*Exit.*

ROSAMUND.

And I will see it. And, father, thou shalt see.

[*Exit.*

ACT V

The Banqueting-hall.

Enter ALBOVINE *and* ROSAMUND.

ALBOVINE.

THIS June makes babes of men; last night I
    deemed
When thou hadst wished me peace as I passed forth
A footfall pressed behind me soft and fast,
And turning toward it I beheld nought: thee
I saw, and Almachildes hard at hand
Turned back toward thee: nought stranger: yet my
    heart
Sprang, and sank back. I laughed against myself,
That manhood should be girlish, when the heat
Burns life half out within us. Even thine eyes,
Like stars before the wind that brings the cloud,
Look fainter. Ere they fill the banquet full
And bid the guests about us where we sit,
Tell me if aught be worse than well with thee.

ROSAMUND.

Nought.

ALBOVINE.

Wilt thou swear it, sweet?

ROSAMUND.

By what thou wilt—

By God and man -- by hell and earth and heaven.

I know what ails thy loyal heart of love   .

And binds thy tongue for fear to bid me know.

The cup we drank of when we feasted last

Tastes bitter on it yet. Thou wilt not bid me

Pledge thee therein again. If I bid thee,

Pledge me thou shalt—and seal thy pardon.

ALBOVINE.

Be not

Too sweet for woman.

ROSAMUND.

Cross me not in this.

ALBOVINE.

Mine old fast friend Narsetes hath my word

Plighted. All funeral reverence shall inter

The royal relic, and all thought therewith

Of strife between thy father's child and me

Or less than love and honour.

ROSAMUND.

                     Nay, my lord,

Let the dead thing live as a lifelong sign

Of perfect plight in love and union. This

Were no dishonour done to fatherhood

But honour shown to wedlock. Here is spread

The feast, the bride-feast of my love and thine,

Whereat the cup of death shall serve our lips

To drink forgetfulness of all but love.

Herein thou shalt not thwart me.

ALBOVINE.

                         God forbid.

ROSAMUND.

God hath forbidden : and God shall be obeyed.

Bid thy Narsetes play the cup-bearer,

And I will pour the wine : my hand shall fill

The sacramental draught of love that seals

Our eucharist of wedlock.

ALBOVINE.

Yea, I know

To drink with thee is even to drink with God.

Thou art good as any God was ever.

ROSAMUND.

Ay?

We know not till we die.

ALBOVINE.

Thou art wise and true

As ever maid was born of the oldworld north

In the oldworld years of legend. Bid Narsetes

Bring thee the chalice : thou shalt mix the draught

Whence we will drink life, if true love be life,

Even from the lipless mouth of bone that speaks

Death.   •

ROSAMUND.

I will mix it well with honey and herb

Sweet as the mead our fathers drank, and dreamed

Their gods so drank in heaven—draughts deep and

strong

As life is strong and death is deep. I go

To bid Narsetes hither.   [*Exit.*

ALBOVINE.

Nay, by God,

Whoever God be, never Christ or Thor

Beheld or blessed a nobler wife, whose love

Was found through proof of purity by fire

More like our northern stars and snows and suns,

And sane in strong sufficiency of soul

As womanhood by godhead from the womb

Elected and exalted.

Enter NARSETES.

NARSETES.

King, thy wife

Hath given me back thy message given her.

ALBOVINE.

Ay?

And thou hast given her back my cup, then?

NARSETES.

King,

I have given it. Loth to give it if I were,

Ye know: she knows as thou: thou knowest as she.

ALBOVINE.

What ails thee to distaste thy duty? Man,

Thou shouldst be glad, being loyal. Knowest thou not

Her will it was that we should pledge therein

To-night, this hour, our lifelong love, and seal it

More surely so than priest or prayer can seal?

NARSETES.

Her will it was, I know, not thine. I would

Thou hadst not yielded up to hers thy will.

ALBOVINE.

Thou liest: I have not yielded it: I have given

Love, willing as the springtide sea gives up

Her will to the eastern sea-wind's.

NARSETES.

                                    Love should give

No more than love should crave of love: and this

Is such a gift as hate might crave of death

Or priests of God when angered.

ALBOVINE.

                     Hark thee, man.

Thou art old, and when I loved thee first and found

        thee

My lord and leader down the ways of war,

My master born by right of manfulness

And steersman through the surf of battle, time

Gaped as a gulf between us: sire and son

We might be: now I bid thee hold thy peace,

Lest all these memories perish, and their death

Give life more strong than theirs to wrath, and leave

        thee

Shelterless as a waif of the air when storm .

Drives bird and beast to deathward. What I bade thee

I bid thee do, and leave me.

NARSETES.

                   King, I go.   [*Exit.*

ALBOVINE.

What, have I played the Berserk with my friend?

So should not kings. What meant he? Men wax old,

And age eats out the natural sense of love

Which gives the soul sight of such nobler things

As trust may see by grace of truth more fair

Than doubt would fear to dream of. Rosamund

Knows more by might of faith and love than he.

And yet I would, and yet I would not, fool

As even in mine own eyes I am, she had not

Given me this proof, desired of me this sign,

How clear her soul is toward me save of love,

To attest her pardon of me. Would it were

Sunrise to-morrow!

> *Enter* ALMACHILDES *and* HILDEGARD.

Whence come these, to bring

Sunrise about me? Nay, I bade you be

Here. Does thy memory too not fail thee, boy,

Burnt out by stress of summer?

ALMACHILDES.

No.

ALBOVINE.

Nor hers?

HILDEGARD.

How might it, king? Thou art good to us.

ALBOVINE.

All things born
Seem good to lovers in their spring of love,
And all men should be. Maiden, God doth well
To give us foresight of the sight of heaven
By looking in such eyes as love like thine
Kindles and veils for love's sake. Fain was I
To see my boy's bride and her bridegroom here
Before the feast broke in on us, and bless
Their love with mine—if mine be blessing.

HILDEGARD.

Sire,
As the earth gives thanks in spring for the April sun
I would and cannot yield you thanks for this.

ALMACHILDES.

I cannot thank at all. I cannot thank
God.

ALBOVINE.

Art thou mazed with love? For her thou canst not
Thank God? What feverish doubt of love or life
Crazes or cramps thy spirit?

ALMACHILDES.

I cannot say.

My heart, if any heart be left in me,

Is as it was not thankless: yet, my king,

I know not how to thank thee.

ALBOVINE.

Thank me not:

I did not bid thee thank me. Love thy love,

And God be with you: so may God be found

Thankworthier. Keep some heart in thee awhile

For God's and her sake.

ALMACHILDES.

All I may I will.

Re-enter ROSAMUND, *followed by* NARSETES *and*

Guests.

ALBOVINE.

Sit, friends and warriors: thou, my boy, next me,

And by my wife thy bride. This night, that leaves

But two days more for June to burn and live,

Plights with my queen's troth mine in life and death

This last one time for ever, in the cup

Whence none shall drink hereafter. Not in scorn,

Sirs, but in honour now the draught is pledged

Between us, ere this relic stand enshrined

And hallowed as a saint's on the altar. Queen,

I drink to thee.

ROSAMUND.

    I thank thee. Good Narsetes,

Give him the chalice. Women slain by fire

Thirst not as I to pledge thee.

          [*As* ALBOVINE *is about to take the cup,*

          ALMACHILDES *rises and stabs him.*

ALBOVINE.

        Thou, my boy? [*Dies.*

ROSAMUND.

I. But he hears not. Now, my warrior guests,

I drink to the onward passage of his soul

Death. Had my hand turned coward or played me false,

This man that is my hand, and less than I

And less than he bloodguilty, this my death

Had been my husband's: now he has left it me.

[*Drinks.*

How innocent are all but he and I

No time is mine to tell you. Truth shall tell.

I pardon thee, my husband: pardon me.   [*Dies.*

NARSETES.

Let none make moan. This doom is none of man's.

THE END

www.ingramcontent.com/pod-product-compliance
Lightning Source LLC
Chambersburg PA
CBHW032349020726
47499CB00008B/2677